Samuel French Acting Edi

Old Stock:
A Refugee Love Story

Created by Christian Barry,
Ben Caplan, and
Hannah Moscovitch

Original songs by Ben Caplan
and Christian Barry

Text by Hannah Moscovitch

ǁSAMUEL FRENCHǁ

FOR PRODUCTION ENQUIRIES

UNITED STATES AND CANADA
info@concordtheatricals.com
1-866-979-0447

UNITED KINGDOM AND EUROPE
licensing@concordtheatricals.co.uk
020-7054-7200

Each title is subject to availability from Concord Theatricals Corp., depending upon country of performance. Please be aware that *OLD STOCK: A REFUGEE LOVE STORY* may not be licensed by Concord Theatricals Corp. in your territory. Professional and amateur producers should contact the nearest Concord Theatricals Corp. office or licensing partner to verify availability.

OLD STOCK: A REFUGEE LOVE STORY was originally produced by 2b theatre company in co-production with the National Arts Centre at The Waiting Room in Halifax, Nova Scotia, Canada on May 4, 2017. It was first produced in the United States at 59E59 Theaters, in New York, New York on March 8, 2018. The production was directed by Christian Barry ,with sets and lights by Louisa Adamson and Christian Barry, sound by Jordan Palmer, Graham Scott, Christian Barry, and Ben Caplan, and costumes by Carly Beamish. The assistant director was Laura Vingoe-Cram, the voice and speech coach was Susan Stackhouse. The production stage manager was Louisa Adamson. The cast and musicians were as follows:

THE WANDERER . . . . Ben Caplan
CHAYA, Violin . . . . Mary Fay Coady
CHAIM, Woodwinds . . . . Christopher Weatherstone
Keyboard and Accordion . . . . Graham Scott
Drumset . . . . Jamie Kronick

Thanks to The Citadel Theatre and the Theatre Arts Residency program at Banff Centre for their contributions to the development of *OLD STOCK: A REFUGEE LOVE STORY*, and to our co-production partners at the National Arts Centre.

CHARACTERS

THE WANDERER – Guitar, Banjo, Harmonica, Vocals.
CHAYA – Violin, Vocals.
CHAIM – Clarinet, Saxophone, Spoons, Vocals.
ACCORDIONIST – Keyboard, Accordion, Vocals.
DRUMMER – Drums, Vocals.

SETTING

In your city

TIME

Now

AUTHORS' NOTES

Chaya and Chaim speak with Jewish inflection.

NOTE FROM HANNAH MOSCOVITCH

The text of *OLD STOCK: A REFUGEE LOVE STORY* was inspired by the lives of my great-grandparents, Chaya Yankovitch and Chaim Moscovitch. They fled from Romania to Canada in 1908. When there have been gaps in my knowledge of actual events, I have taken artistic liberties. For instance, I do not know the full story of how my great-grandfather Chaim Moscovitch's family died in Romania. And because I have often been working from incomplete information, I have discovered over the course of this project that I have parts of my family's history wrong. In two instances, I decided to leave my inaccuracies in the text. I originally thought that Chaya was older than Chaim; I later found out from a census that they were in fact the same age. And I believed that Sam Moscovitch, my grandfather, was the oldest child in the family. He was in fact the second child: his sister Mary (Michal) Moscovitch was the first born.

(The theatre is empty except for strands of twinkly lights hanging from the lighting grid and extending out into the theatre, and a massive shipping container, the type you'd see on an industrial dock. Smoke curls around the shipping container, atmospheric.)

(The show starts when the trap door at the top of the shipping container opens. **THE WANDERER** *appears. He launches straight into the first song.)*

[MUSIC NO. 01 "THE TRAVELLER'S CURSE"]

THE WANDERER.

I HAVE BEEN LIBELLED AS A WANDERER
THIS IS NOT THE CASE
I HAVE A HOME
IT'S JUST THAT IT'S AN INCONVENIENT PLACE RIGHT NOW

"NONE IS TOO MANY OF THAT KIND,"
I OVERHEAR YOU SAY
YOU MAKE SOME MARKINGS ON THE PAGE
AND STAMP AND SEAL MY FATE

I REGRET NOW TO INFORM YOU WHO REFUSE TO AID MY PLIGHT:
BAD LUCK WILL COME TO THOSE WHO DENY THE TRAVELLERS THEIR RIGHTS

*(***THE WANDERER*** disappears back into the shipping container. The front of the shipping container opens out to reveal the rest of the performers – a drummer, an accordionist, a violinist, and a clarinetist. A raised platform that acts as a tiny stage folds down out of the shipping container –* **THE WANDERER** *often*

performs from here. The shipping container is packed full of relics: old carpets, maps, suitcases, a brass samovar, and musical instruments and gear. The objects and décor in the shipping container look like a mix of modern touring equipment that would travel with any rock band and the belongings of turn-of-the-century refugees. All performers wear period clothes, but this isn't Anne of Green Gables. *The period costumes are sexy, stylish, cabaret, and add to the atmosphere of fallen old world decadence, of carnival. Affixed to the upper edges of the shipping container on both sides are two wooden signs in white paint. The left one reads "OLD" and the right one reads "STOCK." Note:* **THE WANDERER** *is the only performer who exits and enters the shipping container – all the other performers remain inside for the duration (except to open and close its doors).)*

WHO CAN DENY YOUR MORAL RIGHT TO PROSPERITY AND ORDER?
YOU FELL OUT OF YOUR MOTHER ON THE CORRECT SIDE OF THE BORDER
AND THAT MOTHER-FALL GIVES YOU ALL OF THIS POWER OVER ME TODAY
BUT THERE ARE FORCES IN THIS WORLD THAT COULD MAKE ALL THAT FALL AWAY IN A SECOND

ALL OF MY PITY UPON YOU!
ALL OF MY PITY UPON YOU!
MY LUCK CAN ONLY GET BETTER;
YOURS IS BOUND TO BE WORSE
NOW I SEE IT UPON YOU
THE TRAVELLER'S CURSE

LA DA DA DEE
DA DA DA
LA DA BA DA DA
BA DA DA BA DA DEE

LA DA DEE YA
LA DA DA DEE
LA DA DA DA
LA DA DA DEE
LA DA DA DA
DA DA DA DA

    (Instrumental break.)

DON'T BE MISLED AND THINK THIS CURSE
IS MINE TO MAKE OR LIFT
YOU PUT IT ON YOURSELF;
IT'S NOT MY PLACE
TO BEND AND SIFT
YOUR CONSCIENCE AND YOUR CHARACTER
YOUR LUCK IS ALL YOUR OWN
GOOD LUCK WITH THAT
I LEAVE YOU NOW
BUT YOU'LL NEVER BE ALONE

WITH ALL OF MY PITY UPON YOU!
ALL OF MY PITY UPON YOU!
MY LUCK CAN ONLY GET BETTER;
YOURS IS BOUND TO BE WORSE
NOW I SEE IT UPON YOU
THE TRAVELLER'S CURSE

Intermezzo One

(**THE WANDERER**, *a rabbinical Tom Waits, a profane Chagall, grabs a microphone and speaks directly to the audience.*)

THE WANDERER. *(To the audience.)* Welcome, welcome, hello audience!

We made it! You made it! Others were not so lucky.

[MUSIC NO. 01A "WELCOME, WELCOME!"]

Let me tell you a story.

Tonight I arrived in New York* by boat.

Mmm actually it was more of a *dinghy* and the water was choppy – I got a few of mouthfuls of salt water – and I thought "this is a shitty way to travel."

That's a lie!

Tonight, I arrived in New York* by train

High speed train, Nova Scotia to New York*, only thirty-three hours.

That is also a lie!

I took a rented SUV – it had seat warmers that put a tingle in my undercarriage.

That is *not* a lie.

Okay so this Yiddishkeit music thing we're doing…

It's about immigrants and Jews and it's about refugees and in particular Jewish refugees

But we hope you can see something of yourself in it…

Maybe?

But maybe not

But maybe…?

After all, we all come out of the same box.

(*Beat.*)

We all, sometimes, find ourselves pounding on the door, hoping to be let in, even if it's the door to…the human heart.

---

* Insert the name of the town where the show is happening tonight. Adjust the time / distance by train accordingly.

(Beat.)

[MUSIC NO. 01B "ARE YOU FROM ROMANIA?"]

Okay, lemme tell you a little thing that's true.

It's 1908 and we're in a building called Pier Two

In a little harbour town on the edge of the North Atlantic

Called Halifax.

> (**THE WANDERER** *gestures – the wooden sign with the word "STOCK" painted on it in white lettering is flipped over to reveal the world "HALIFAX."*)

A lot of people are crammed together who've just arrived

A little like this audience only none of them have showered

Fathers smoking

Mothers nursing

Children wandering aimlessly through the swirling human mass

A restless hope in the air as blank-eyed bureaucrats stamp papers

It's not the most romantic of places but...

To one particular man and woman?

Doesn't fucking matter.

> *(Lights shift.)*

Scene One

(CHAIM and CHAYA stand side-by-side, with their suitcases, to suggest a secondary medical inspection waiting area at Pier Two, in Halifax. CHAIM notices CHAYA. Then he can't help himself: he keeps glancing at her. Note: stagings are simple, and the contents of the shipping container remain visible throughout as do the other performers.)

CHAIM. Are you from Romania?

CHAYA. I'm from Romania.

CHAIM. Romania, I thought so! But you weren't on the boat...?

CHAYA. We came through Russia.

CHAIM. Ahn! Ahn!

(She coughs.)

Good boat? Bad boat?

CHAYA. I don't know. I don't have another boat to compare it to.

CHAIM. How was the food?

CHAYA. Enh.

(Beat.)

CHAIM. What's your name?

CHAYA. Chaya.

CHAIM. Chaya?! *(Introducing himself.)* Chaim! Chaim Moscovitch.

(They smile a little.)

By yourself, on the boat?

CHAYA. No, with... My mother, Rachel Yankovitch, and my father, Yankel Yankovitch, and my sister, Sarah Gittel and her husband Marku, and my sister Devorah Leah and her husband Benjamin, and their daughter Reba, and my sister Ethel Miriam, and my brother,

Shmuel Moishe and his wife Talia and their son Avrum, and my brother Menashe and his wife Feige and their son Isser, and my brother Machel and his wife Yetta and their daughters, Shira and Sarah.

> *(Beat.)*

Your family?

> *(Beat.)*

Sickness?

CHAIM. Pogrom.

CHAYA. Anh. Anh. May no more harm befall you.

CHAIM. Amen.

> *(Beat.)*

I have a rash on my arm, that's why I'm in this line.

> *(**CHAYA** looks at his gross rash with some interest.)*

CHAYA. They think this is Typhus? This isn't Typhus.

CHAIM. What is it, then?

CHAYA. A rash.

CHAIM. You've had Typhus?

CHAYA. No, my husband, he…died of it. On the road to Russia. He had a rash come up, but it didn't look like that.

CHAIM. May no more harm befall you.

CHAYA. Amen, amen.

> *(**CHAYA** opens the locket that's hanging around her neck.)*

That's Yochay.

CHAIM. Handsome.

CHAYA. I thought so.

> *(Beat: **CHAIM** grasping for what to say now…)*

CHAIM. Do you have…a rash, or…something other than…a rash or…?

CHAYA. I have a cough, and one of my sisters died of Tuberculosis. It's in our papers. They heard me coughing, they said, "She's got Tuberculosis, like her sister," but I don't: I have a cough.

(*To prove the point,* **CHAYA** *coughs.*)

CHAIM. How do you like Canada?

CHAYA. I...?

CHAIM. *I* like it.

CHAYA. You've been outside?

CHAIM. No.

CHAYA. So what do you like? You like this building?

CHAIM. There's a window.

(**CHAIM** *gestures.*)

There are trees. Sky. Ocean.

(*Beat.*)

Birds.

(*Beat.*)

I like meeting you. The new world: not so formal.

(**CHAYA**'s *alarmed by this very direct and open style of flirting.*)

CHAYA. We're not planning to stay, we're here until Romania's...not so bad, then we go back.

CHAIM. All of you?

CHAYA. Some will stay. My brothers? Not me. My husband died in Russia. I don't want an ocean between me and his grave.

(*Lights shift to* **THE WANDERER.**)

[MUSIC NO. 02 "YOU'VE ARRIVED"]

THE WANDERER.

YOU'VE ARRIVED
THAT MUCH IS CLEAR
GOD KNOWS WHERE YOU'RE COMING FROM
BUT NOW YOU'RE HERE

JUST RELAX, BUT NOT TOO MUCH
I NEED YOUR COOPERATION
TO ENSURE A GENTLE TOUCH

> (**THE WANDERER** *opens a suitcase, and pulls out a couple of cloth dolls. He manipulates them during the below verses, making them talk, bending them over, making them shake with fear, and ultimately throwing them over the edge of the shipping container.*)

I WILL NEED A VOLUNTEER
MAYBE TWO TO GET US GOING
THERE'S A LOT TO GET THROUGH HERE
THANK YOU SIR
AND THANK YOU MA'AM
STEP RIGHT UP
FOR YOUR EXAM!
YOU WILL HELP TO DEMONSTRATE
FOR ALL EIGHT HUNDRED FORTY-EIGHT

YOU'VE SURVIVED
SO HAVE NO FEAR
YOU HAVE TRAVELLED LONG AND FAR
BUT NOW THE JOURNEY'S END IS NEAR

YOU SAY "THANK YOU"
"I'M IN YOUR DEBT"
I WOULD LIKE TO SAY YOU'RE WELCOME
BUT THAT'S NOT ESTABLISHED YET

WE MUST MOVE THROUGH SOME FORMALITIES
PRESCRIBED BY THE BUREAUCRACY
UPON WHICH WE MUST ALL AGREE
BEFORE I CAN SAY THAT YOU'RE FREE

BEFORE THE RIGHT TO EARN A DOLLAR
A QUICK LOOK TO CHECK FOR CHOLERA
FORMALITY I'M CERTAIN;
"COULD I STEP BEHIND A CURTAIN?"

THERE'S NO TIME FOR MODESTY!
ANOTHER BOAT ARRIVES AT THREE;

THERE'S CHICKEN POX, APPENDICITIS,
MEASLES, POLIO, BRONCHITIS
TYPHUS, AND RHEUMATIC FEVER;
ALL THE DOCTORS HERE ARE EAGER!

NOW LET'S TRY A COUPLE POSES
TURN AROUND AND TOUCH YOUR TOESES

AND OF COURSE, THIS POSE EXPOSES
PLACES THAT DON'T SMELL LIKE ROSES

"BUT FOR MODESTY GOD CHOSE US!"
I'VE NO TIME FOR BOOKS OF MOSES

BEFORE THE FRESH AIR HITS YOUR NOSES
WE MUST TEST FOR TUBERCULOSIS

JUST A LITTLE DEGRADATION
BEFORE YOU CAN JOIN OUR NATION
YOU ACCEPT OUR INVITATION
CONDITIONAL ON A VERIFIED AND CERTIFIED
     CERTIFICATE
OF SANITATION
Yes! Yes! Marvelous! It's spinning, it's spinning!

> (**THE WANDERER** *dances across the stage. He
> plays a harmonica to make the sound of a
> train whistle, while the drums suggest a turn-
> of-the-century steam engine slowing down
> and pulling into a station.* **THE WANDERER**
> *reaches up and flips over the painted
> wooden sign with the word "OLD" painted
> on it in white lettering to reveal the word
> "MONTREAL.")*

> (**THE WANDERER** *watches as lights shift to the
> next scene.)*

Scene Two

[MUSIC NO. 02A "DO YOU WANT TO MARRY ME?"]

(1908. This is **CHAYA**'s *new family home in Montreal: an ornate brass samovar, heavy air.* **CHAIM** *enters, sees* **CHAYA**.*)*

CHAIM. You – you're very – you're how I remember you.

(Beat.)

Do you remember *me*?

CHAYA. *(Simultaneous.)* Chaim –

CHAIM. *(Simultaneous.)* Chaim Moscovitch – yes! I was at shul, I heard your father's name, I said: "Yankel Yankovitch with a daughter Chaya?" I said: "What are the chances! I've met your daughter: she was the first thing I saw in Canada!"

(Beat.)

Thank you for agreeing to this meeting with me.

CHAYA. You're in good health?

CHAIM. *(Nodding.)* And you? Your cough...?

*(***CHAYA** *coughs.)*

How do you like Montreal?

*(***CHAYA** *shrugs.)*

CHAYA. Not Romania.

CHAIM. No, not Romania! But cold like Romania. My landlady, she asked me: "You're from a Northern country: how did you keep warm?"

(Beat.)

I said: "Vodka."

(Beat. Then in a lower voice, a more serious tone.)

We didn't keep warm, is the truth.

CHAYA. What kind of a wife are you looking for?

> *(Beat.)*

CHAIM. You!

> *(Beat.)*

CHAYA. What's your work?

CHAIM. I'd like other work. On the railway...? I have factory work.

CHAYA. Anh. Factory. How old are you?

CHAIM. Nineteen. You're older?

CHAYA. Twenty-four.

> *(Beat.)*

You should find a young bride: you're a good looking boy –

CHAIM. I could, but... I don't know why, but... I think this is right.

> *(Beat: they both blush.)*

CHAYA. I went hungry for a year and my skin sagged, and I've a couple of broken teeth, on the bottom. I take a lot of sugar in my tea, so much you'll say: "Chaya that's not tea it's sludge!!!" but that's how I like it. My father will have told you what a good wife I am, but I have bad qualities. I have a temper, and my cooking's not so good – you're nodding, why are you nodding?

CHAIM. Your father told me about the cooking.

CHAYA. *(Surprised.)* He did?

CHAIM. Too much salt.

CHAYA. *(Bristling.)* He said that?!

> *(They're getting distracted so* **CHAIM** *quickly pivots.)*

CHAIM. I – please – I...do you want to marry me?

> *(Beat.)*

CHAYA. My father likes you.

CHAIM. Your father likes me: good, good. Do you like me?

(Beat.)

I'm young.

CHAYA. This I don't mind.

(Pause: they look at each other. There's a sexual charge. But then **CHAYA** *looks down or away.)*

(Formal.) On the question of our marriage I will be guided by my father.

*(***CHAIM*** *looks at her for a long moment, considering. Then he shakes his head.)*

CHAIM. *(Almost to himself, a decision.)* It's not enough.

*(***CHAIM*** *downs his tea and stands.)*

You'll tell your father it won't work out between us?

*(***CHAYA*** *thinks for a second, gazing at him. She goes to the samovar and pours* **CHAIM** *more tea. The samovar tap squeaks in the silence.* **CHAYA** *holds out the tea cup to* **CHAIM.***)*

CHAYA. Sit. Drink.

(Lights shift to **THE WANDERER.***)*

Intermezzo Two

THE WANDERER. *(To the audience.)* So
A man and a woman
Leave a country full of wolves for a country full of
actual wolves
They meet
One falls in love
And now...
A new life...?
But the trouble is...
Outside of Bucharest there are fields of cornflowers
and yarrow, ox-eye daisies, wild thyme.
When Chaya was little she rolled around in them
When she got older she picked them and gave them to
the boys she liked
There was one boy in particular
Called Yochay
Handsome and tall and...
Fuckable...

> *(Beat.)*

Eminently fuckable.

> *(Beat.)*

Okay so Judaism, it might surprise you to know, is very
positive, very enthusiastic even, about fucking! It's a
mitzvah, a commandment, a blessing, "be fruitful and
multiply" – you know, with your husband or wife. Of
course the Bible says, "Adulterers must be put to death,"
but that's just part of *any sacrificial desert cult,* am I
right?

> *(Beat.)*

And look, the Jewish oral law states that you can't put
anyone to death for the crime of adultery unless there
are at least two witnesses to the crime...so unless you
invite some people over to see your adultery, unless

you have an adultery party, there's a fair amount of rabbinical wiggle-room. There's the Bible, but there's also the oral tradition.

[MUSIC NO. 03 "TRUTH DOESN'T LIVE IN A BOOK"]

(Shift into song intro. Atmospheric dark lights on all the musicians in the shipping container.)

Everybody knows that the Bible is full of wisdom
The Good Book is great!
But a few thousand years of theological disputes and debates have shown that the text was written in such a way that it
(Spoken in rhythm.) INHERENTLY REQUIRES INTENSIVE, RIGOROUS, AND CONSTANT
(Sung.) INTERPRETATION!
Did you know, when the Bible was given
It was delivered along with an oral tradition
Which at the time was expressly forbidden
 TO BE WRITTEN DOWN.
Well – the reason why, I submit, must be
Is that this was to prevent undue rigidity, you see
The Bible is a living work that needs to breathe in order to stay alive.
Now, I hope my approach won't be seen as ham-fisted
And we all know that words get distorted and twisted
But it is my contention that some of the best bits
 WERE NOT WRITTEN DOWN

(Lights on the band are bright now.)

ALWAYS HAVE A BIT OF SALT WITH YOUR TEQUILA
DON'T SMOKE YOUR STASH IF YOU'RE GONNA BE A
    DEALER
TRY TO DRINK AT LEAST EIGHT CUPS OF WATER EVERY
    DAY

ALWAYS KEEP YOUR HOCKEY STICK ON THE ICE

IF YOU WANNA CUT ONCE YOU BETTER MEASURE TWICE
THERE'S NO SUCH THING AS A LUNCH THAT'S REALLY
    FREE

THE WANDERER.	CHAYA & CHAIM.
AN EYE FOR AN	OOH
EYE MEANS FAIR	
COMPENSATION	
IT DOESN'T MEAN TAKE UP	
ARMS WITH ANOTHER	OOH
NATION	
ANYTHING WRITTEN	
DOWN CAN BE TWISTED	
APART	AAH
DON'T BE ASHAMED TO	OOH
TALK ABOUT YOUR	
MENTAL HEALTH	
TRY LOVE YOUR	
NEIGHBOUR LIKE YOU	
LOVE YOURSELF	OOH
THAT ONE'S IN THERE	
BUT IT ALWAYS GETS	AAH
FORGOTTEN	

THE WANDERER, CHAYA & CHAIM.

TRUTH DOESN'T LIVE IN A BOOK
YOU FIND IT IN THE LITTLE SURPRISES
THE GOOD BOOK IS ONLY A LENS TO FOCUS THE VIEW
JUSTICE FOR ALL
IS COMPOSED OF THE UGLIEST COMPROMISES
YOU CAN'T ONLY LOOK AT THE LENS, YOU'VE GOTTA
    LOOK THROUGH

THE WANDERER.

THERE'S NO SUCH THING AS A VIRGIN CONCEPTION
EVERY GOOD RULE HAS A NOTABLE EXCEPTION
DON'T SURROUND YOURSELF WITH FRIENDS WHO ONLY
    AGREE

DON'T COUNT YOUR EGGS BEFORE THEY'RE CHICKEN
ASK FOR CONSENT BEFORE YOU PUT YOUR DICK IN
AIN'T NOTHING WRONG WITH HOMOSEXUALITY

THE WANDERER.	CHAYA & CHAIM.
DON'T GET CAUGHT WITH YOUR PANTS AROUND YOUR ANKLE	OOH
IF YOU WANNA HIDE YOUR MONEY STICK IN A SWISS BANK-LE	OOH
EVERY BANKING SYSTEM NEEDS A LOT OF REGULATION	AAH
NEVER DRAW A PICTURE OF THE PROPHET MOHAMMED	OOH
UNLESS YOU'RE A CARTOONIST AND YOU REALLY, REALLY WANNA	OOH
ILLUSTRATE CULTURAL INSENSITIVITY	EEE

THE WANDERER, CHAYA & CHAIM.
TRUTH DOESN'T LIVE IN A BOOK
YOU FIND IT IN THE LITTLE SURPRISES
THE GOOD BOOK IS ONLY A LENS TO FOCUS THE VIEW

THE WANDERER. *Sing along!*
You'll find the lyrics under your seats!
That's a lie!

THE WANDERER, CHAYA, CHAIM & AUDIENCE.
JUSTICE FOR ALL
IS COMPOSED OF THE UGLIEST COMPROMISES
YOU CAN'T ONLY LOOK AT THE LENS, YOU'VE GOTTA
    LOOK THROUGH

TRUTH DOESN'T LIVE IN A BOOK
YOU FIND IT IN THE LITTLE SURPRISES
THE GOOD BOOK IS ONLY A LENS TO FOCUS THE VIEW
JUSTICE FOR ALL
IS COMPOSED OF THE UGLIEST COMPROMISES

YOU CAN'T ONLY LOOK AT THE LENS, YOU'VE GOTTA
    LOOK THROUGH

    (**THE WANDERER** *sings ad-lib.*)

CHAYA, CHAIM & AUDIENCE.

TRUTH DOESN'T LIVE IN A BOOK
YOU FIND IT IN THE LITTLE SURPRISES
THE GOOD BOOK IS ONLY A LENS TO FOCUS THE VIEW
JUSTICE FOR ALL
IS COMPOSED OF THE UGLIEST COMPROMISES
YOU CAN'T ONLY LOOK AT THE LENS, YOU'VE GOTTA
    LOOK THROUGH

THE WANDERER.

YOU HAVE TO LIVE IN THE WORLD TO GET TO THE TRUTH

    (*Lights shift, grow dim, into "Od Yishama."*)

[MUSIC NO. 04 "OD YISHAMA"]

(*During "Od Yishama,"* **THE WANDERER** *wraps
a tallis around his shoulders.* **CHAYA** *wears a
wedding veil, and* **CHAIM** *is in a traditional
white wedding kittel. They put up strands of
white linen garlands.* **CHAYA** *walks around*
CHAIM *seven times. Then they play their
instruments. The staging is metatheatrical:
the performers are both musicians and their
characters as they play to one another.*)

OD YISHAMA B'AREI YEHUDAH

UVECHUTZOT, UVECHUTZOT YERUSHALAIM:

OD YISHAMA B'AREI YEHUDAH

UVECHUTZOT, UVECHUTZOT YERUSHALAIM:

KOL SASON V'KOL SIMCHAH,
KOL CHATAN V'KOL KALAH.
KOL SASON V'KOL SIMCHAH,
KOL CHATAN V'KOL KALAH.

    (*As the song ends,* **CHAIM** *stamps his foot and
crushes a glass.*)

Scene Three

[MUSIC NO. 04A "YOU WERE YOCHAY'S SECOND CHOICE"]

(**CHAIM** *and* **CHAYA** *glance at each other.*)

CHAIM. Mazel Tov.

CHAYA. Mazel Tov.

> (*Beat.*)

CHAIM. We're alone.

CHAYA. We've been alone before.

CHAIM. Not like this.

CHAYA. My brothers got you drunk.

CHAIM. No.

> (*Beat.*)

It was your father.

CHAYA. You're drunk.

CHAIM. And happy, Chayaleh. Chayaleh, so happy I can feel God.

> (**CHAYA** *can't help herself: she smiles.*)

> (**CHAIM** *leans in to kiss* **CHAYA**, *very close, almost kissing her but then...*)

> (**CHAIM** *pulls back.*)

You know better than me what to do.

CHAYA. Okay well: do something and then we'll see.

> (**CHAIM** *leans in and... This time he kisses* **CHAYA**, *gently and then more passionately.*)

It's good.

CHAIM. It is?

CHAYA. Yes: look, let me – like this:

> (**CHAYA** *kisses him, much harder than he kissed her. The assertive quality of* **CHAYA**'s

sexuality leads **CHAIM** *to ask the below question.)*

CHAIM. Was he…? Was he…good at this…?

CHAYA. Yochay?

CHAIM. Yes: Yochay?

CHAYA. I don't know. I don't have anything to compare him to! He was *Yochay*, / he was –

CHAIM. You have *me* to compare him to.

CHAYA. Okay, so, good, you want me to compare? So, give me something to compare, and then I'll compare!

(*They kiss.*)

CHAIM. What are you thinking?

CHAYA. I'm not thinking: that's the point.

CHAIM. You have thoughts.

CHAYA. They're my thoughts, if I wanted to say them, I'd say them.

CHAIM. I'm your husband: who else are you going to tell your thoughts to?

CHAYA. God.

CHAIM. Tell them to *me*.

(*Beat.*)

Please –

CHAYA. I'm thinking: all this joy you feel? I've felt it once before.

(**CHAYA** *turns away and starts unbuttoning her dress.*)

I put on a wedding dress. I had hopes.

(**CHAYA**'s *in her own world as she says the below.*)

He was…handsome and…tall and…

CHAIM. (*Kindly, as though to free her.*) You know what your father told me? You were Yochay's second choice. He wanted your sister Raba. But she had Tuberculosis, so he took you.

(Beat.)

CHAYA. He...

(Beat.)

CHAIM. Raba with the red hair? Your father told me he liked Raba's hair. You were too plain for him.

(Beat.)

Not a nice man, this Yochay.

(Beat.)

I...! I shouldn't have told you –

CHAYA. May God curse you. May he kill your firstborn son!

(Lights snap over to **THE WANDERER.** *)*

Intermezzo Three

THE WANDERER. *(To the audience.)* Mazel Tov to the newly weds!!!!

As our sages say: a wedding without a band is like a piss without a fart.

Happy music, happy people!

One, two, three...

[MUSIC NO. 05 "THE WANDERER'S BULGAR"]

(During the wedding music, THE WANDERER dances, flinging his legs up in the air, wild, ecstatic, in the old Romanian style. He finds a bottle of vodka and drinks... Then he sits and listens to the virtuosity of the musicians, clapping along, celebrating.)

(At the end of the wedding music.)

L'chaim!

Mazel Tov...!

Happy music! Happy people!

Later on you'll be miserable, that comes for all of us, so good to be happy on your wedding day!

[MUSIC NO. 06 "MINIMUM INTERVALS"]

(The beginning of the "Minimum Intervals" song is played as lights shift to the next scene.)

Scene Four

*(****CHAYA**** brushes out her long hair. ****CHAIM****
hovers nearby. ****CHAYA**** faces away, doesn't
look at him.)*

CHAIM. I have new work, better pay.

(Beat.)

On the trains.

(Beat.)

Eight dollars a week.

(Beat.)

In the engine room, hot work –

CHAYA. Talking, talking: no one's listening.

*(****CHAYA**** takes her hair down.)*

*(****CHAIM**** watches…)*

CHAIM. Your hair…

*(****CHAYA**** turns and gazes at ****CHAIM****. Then she
walks over, takes his hand, puts it on her
hair.)*

CHAYA. You married me, so…here, my hair. Here, touch it,
not red hair like Raba but…!

CHAIM. Sorry.

CHAYA. Here.

CHAIM. Sorry, sorry.

*(Lights snap over to ****THE WANDERER****.)*

THE WANDERER. The minimum intervals for conjugal duties
as prescribed in the Talmud are as follows:

FOR MEN OF INDEPENDENT MEANS EVERY DAY IS WHAT
SHE NEEDS.

LABOURERS IT'S TWICE IS A WEEK, YOU'VE GOT TO MAKE
YOUR LADY SQUEAK.

DONKEY DRIVERS ONCE IN SEVEN, GOTTA SEND YOUR
SPOUSE TO HEAVEN.

SAILORS EVERY HALF A YEAR, IT'S BACK TO PORT YOU'VE
GOT TO STEER.

(Lights shift back to **CHAIM** *and* **CHAYA**.*)*

Scene Five

(CHAYA faces upstage. She's busy doing dishes as CHAIM comes in. CHAYA doesn't look up or acknowledge CHAIM, she continues with her chores as though he's not there. CHAIM holds a brown paper package.)

CHAIM. I got you sugar for your tea, I saw we were out of sugar.

(Beat.)

What did you do today? Anything nice.

(Beat.)

Your father was at shul. He looked well.

(Beat.)

I was thinking of an English name for myself. Charles? Harry? Chaim...Harry? No, not good? Kevin?

(Beat.)

I'll go practice my English.

(CHAYA gets up abruptly, goes to him, starts to undress him.)

What...? What are you doing?

(CHAYA undresses him, pulling open his buttons.)

No, Chaya, what are you doing?

CHAYA. I want a baby.

(Beat.)

CHAIM. So do I?

CHAYA. So?

(CHAYA resumes pulling off his clothes.)

CHAIM. I – no!

CHAYA. Why not?

CHAIM. I – I don't – I – don't know what's happening – I'm sorry, I'm sorry – I shouldn't have said what I said about Yochay –

CHAYA. You're sorry: so, good, show me you're sorry.

> *(Beat.)*

> (**CHAIM** *is upset and confused but doesn't know how to say no.*)

CHAIM. Alright.

CHAYA. Good.

> *(As* **CHAYA** *rips his shirt down, mechanical and rough, lights snap us to* **THE WANDERER.***)*

THE WANDERER.

ACCORDING TO THE OLD TRADITION
A JEWISH HUSBAND IS FORBIDDEN
TO GO FOR TOO LONG WITHOUT SPENDING
TIME ON NETHER-REGION TENDING

FOR MEN OF INDEPENDENT MEANS EVERY DAY IS WHAT SHE NEEDS
LABOURERS IT'S TWICE IS A WEEK, YOU'VE GOT TO MAKE YOUR LADY SQUEAK
DONKEY DRIVERS ONCE IN SEVEN, GOTTA SEND YOUR SPOUSE TO HEAVEN
FOR SAILORS EVERY HALF A YEAR, IT'S BACK TO PORT YOU'VE GOT TO STEER

HER PLEASURE IS YOUR OBLIGATION, IF SHE GIVES THE INVITATION
HAS THE RIGHT OF COURSE TO SAY SHE'S NOT QUITE IN THE MOOD TO PLAY
CONSENT IS DE RIGUEUR, YOU'VE ALWAYS GOTTA CHECK WITH HER
THE POINT IS HUMAN BEINGS AS SUCH NEED A LITTLE LOVING TOUCH

FOR MEN OF INDEPENDENT MEANS EVERY DAY IS WHAT SHE NEEDS
LABOURERS IT'S TWICE IS A WEEK, YOU'VE GOT TO MAKE YOUR LADY SQUEAK

DONKEY DRIVERS ONCE IN SEVEN, GOTTA SEND YOUR
SPOUSE TO HEAVEN

SAILORS EVERY HALF A YEAR, IT'S BACK TO PORT YOU'VE
GOT TO STEER

HER PLEASURE IS YOUR OBLIGATION, IF SHE GIVES THE
INVITATION

HAS THE RIGHT OF COURSE TO SAY SHE'S NOT QUITE IN
THE MOOD TO PLAY

CONSENT IS STILL ALWAYS DE RIGUEUR, YOU'VE ALWAYS
GOTTA CHECK WITH HER

THE POINT IS HUMAN BEINGS AS SUCH NEED A LITTLE
LOVING TOUCH

FOR MEN OF INDEPENDENT MEANS EVERY DAY IS WHAT
SHE NEEDS

LABOURERS IT'S TWICE IS A WEEK, YOU'VE GOT TO MAKE
YOUR LADY SQUEAK

DONKEY DRIVERS ONCE IN SEVEN, GOTTA SEND YOUR
SPOUSE TO HEAVEN

SAILORS EVERY HALF A YEAR, IT'S BACK TO PORT YOU'VE
GOT TO STEER

HER PLEASURE IS YOUR OBLIGATION, IF SHE GIVES THE
INVITATION

HAS THE RIGHT OF COURSE TO SAY SHE'S NOT QUITE IN
THE MOOD TO PLAY

CONSENT IS DE RIGUEUR, YOU'VE ALWAYS GOTTA CHECK
WITH HER

EVERY HUMAN BEING AS SUCH NEEDS A LITTLE LOVING
TOUCH

THE POINT IS HUMAN BEINGS AS SUCH NEED A LITTLE
LOVING TOUCH

EVERY HUMAN BEING AS SUCH NEEDS A LITTLE LOVING
TOUCH

EVERY HUMAN BEING AS SUCH NEEDS A LITTLE LOVING
AHHH

*(The band suggests sex. In particular, it's
the clarinet making the bed squeak and
eventually imitating sexual vocalizations.*

The drums also accelerate, the violin trills, and the accordion heaves and moans, all leading to a boisterous climax. Then the clarinet sounds suggests the denouement and fatigue post-sex. Finally, lights shift to **THE WANDERER.***)*

Intermezzo Four

[MUSIC NO. 06A "KNOW EACH OTHER"]

THE WANDERER. So our man and woman have
    Finally
    Finally
    Had the opportunity to
    Know each other
    In the Biblical sense
    You know?
    Adult naptime
    You know?
    Amorous congress
    Being intimate
    Banana in the fruit salad
    No?
    Beard-splitting
    Belly-bumping
    Bouncy-bouncy
    Interior dick-orating

> (**THE WANDERER** *taps the mic as though the comprehension problem is because the audience can't hear him.*)

Batter-dipping the corn dog
Bringing an al dente noodle to the spaghetti house
Cattle-prodding the oyster ditch with the lap rocket
Cleaning the cobwebs with the womb broom
Doing squat thrusts in the cucumber patch
Doing the horizontal greased-weasel tango
Forbidden polka
Four-legged foxtrot
Are you following me?
Getting down
Getting it on

Getting some
Getting the Twinkie stinky

(Beat.)

Going crab fishing in the Dead Sea
Gland-to-gland combat
Harpooning the salty longshoreman
Parking the beef bus in Tuna Town
Playing with the box the kid came in
Praying with the knees upwards
Roughing up the suspect
Rubbing the fun bits
Rummaging in the root cellar
Do I have to spell it out for you?!
Scragging
Screwing
Scrogging
Scromping
Scrumping
Shaboinking
Shafting
Shagging
Shtupping
Shampooing the wookie
Taking ol' One-Eye to the optometrist
Come on people!

(Beat.)

Okay so even though it's not a
Good marriage
They're trying to have a baby
So maybe...?

[MUSIC NO. 06B "A CRACK OPENS UP"]

He's got good work good pay they're in a country where
no one's trying to murder them in their beds

So maybe...?

They're both good people wouldn't you say?

He's handsome she's pretty

So maybe...?

But maybe not.

After all, they come from a long line

From Sarah to Leah to Jezebel

Of preparing for a worst that usually comes.

Can these people be happy?

They're so out of practice

These are chosen people, of course, but what, you might ask, have they been chosen for?

>*(The lights shift.)*

>*(**CHAIM** is onstage now, experiencing what **THE WANDERER** describes.)*

When Chaim goes to a cinema with some friends from synagogue they're told

"Gentiles only"

And of course of course they sound Romanian and of course with more pogroms there are more Jews fleeing to Canada

Chaim sees it in the newspaper

In the Montreal Herald this morning

"Old Stock Canadians soon to be overrun by the Semitic Hordes!"

Standing outside the cinema Chaim thinks to himself

This big cold country doesn't want him to see a movie?

Okay so: no movie

And then a crack opens up

>*(Lights shift. **CHAIM** is in Romania.)*

And from so many miles away he can see the smoke

He gets off the train at Brasov

Snow's falling

There's no commotion it must have happened hours
ago
The butcher's shop is burned and on one of the hooks
hangs the butcher's son

(The cymbals ring, jarring.)

Along a side street a child lies facedown in the snow
In the town square corpses are being laid out
Chaim vomits a couple of times then starts to run
He sees the synagogue its blackened beams have fallen
in
Windows on his street are shattered and
The front door of his house stands open
In the front room he finds his mother

(Pause.)

And three of his brothers

(Pause.)

In the kitchen he finds his father
The back door is open
He goes towards it but
He hears a sound
It's his father moving
Chaim goes back and pulls his father up
Wipes his mouth
Watches as his father points to the back door and says:
"your brother"
Outside Chaim finds his smallest brother
Four years old
Curled up in the snow
His head is

(The cymbals ring, jarring.)

Chaim kneels down and
He's still warm

*(**CHAIM** holds his arms up as though there's a child in them.)*

Chaim picks him up, turns and looks into the eyes of God

*(**THE WANDERER** and **CHAIM** turn and look at each other directly, in the eyes.)*

(A charismatic moment.)

*(Then **CHAIM** lowers his arms, and looks around himself, dazed.)*

Chaim blinks

The sun is bright

He looks around

He's standing on the sidewalk outside a cinema in Montreal.

(Lights shift straight into "Plough the Shit.")

[MUSIC NO. 07 "PLOUGH THE SHIT"]

THE WORLD IS AN OVERFLOWING GUTTER
IT BUBBLES WITH A BRINE OF SHIT AND BLOOD
AND THOSE WHO KEEP THEIR EYES UPON THE HEAVENS
ARE THE ONES WHO'LL WIND UP FACE DOWN IN THE
    MUD

IT'S EASY TO SPEAK OF GRAND AMBITIONS
IT'S EASY TO PRETEND YOU'RE INNOCENT
BUT LEST YOU GET DISTRACTED BY THE SUFF'RING OF
    YOUR SISTER
BEING PRACTICAL AND TRYING TO PAY THE RENT

HEAVEN HAS BEEN PROMISED TO THE RIGHTEOUS,
HELL'S AN OVER-POPULATED PIT
PURGATORY'S GIVEN TO THE DREAMERS
BUT THE WORLD BELONGS TO THOSE WHO PLOUGH THE
    SHIT

THERE'S A SPECIAL PLACE IN HELL FOR FANCY TALKERS
THERE'S A SPECIAL PLACE IN HEAVEN FOR THE WHORES

THERE'S A THRONE RESERVED FOR THOSE WITH GOOD
    IDEAS
STOLEN BY THE DEMAGOGUES WHO WANT IT MORE

THE FLOWERS AND THE LACES IN THE MARKET
ARE ALL PURCHASED BY THE PEDDLERS OF THE FLESH
BUT THOSE WHO BRING RELIEF AND CARNAL PLEASURE
SOMETIMES SERVE THE NEEDS OF MANKIND FOR THE
    BEST

CAST OFF THE LIMITATIONS OF THE RIGHTEOUS,
THERE ARE GOOD DEEDS ONLY DEVILS CAN COMMIT
LET US DANCE BETWEEN THE TEARDROPS OF THE
    ANGELS
FOR THE WORLD BELONGS TO THOSE WHO PLOUGH THE
    SHIT

    *(**THE WANDERER** picks up a megaphone and
    speaks into it over the music.)*

"Throughout this campaign, I have been promoting a unified Canadian identity that is based on historic Canadian values. Progressives, the fake media, and even some on the right have dismissed my policy: that all visitors, all immigrants, and all refugees to Canada must have a face-to-face interview with a trained immigration officer. We must screen for Canadian values!"*

THE DEAD BECOME THE EMPERORS OF MEMORY
THE SAINTS HAVE ALL BEEN EATEN BY THE WORMS
THE LIVING HAVE THE RIGHT TO TWIST THE FUTURE
AND THE SINNERS ALL HAVE PRACTICAL CONCERNS

THERE'S SENTINELS WITH RIFLES ON THE BORDER
ALL THE PRETENSES OF CHARITY ARE SWEPT
BUT LET'S NOT TALK OF SLIPPING INTO NIGHTMARE
FOR THE DAY IS WON BY THOSE WHO HAVEN'T SLEPT

SO THROW AWAY THE VESTMENTS OF THE RIGHTEOUS,
MAKE SURE THE BODY ARMOUR SNUGLY FITS

---

* This speech is loosely inspired by Canadian campaign speeches given in 2017.

THE SOULS HAVE TAKEN FLIGHT NOW FROM THE
    BIRDHOUSE
AND THE WORLD BELONGS TO THOSE WHO PLOUGH THE
    SHIT

    (Lights shift.)

    (A musical interlude connects the two songs.)

[MUSIC NO. 08 "NOW IS THE QUIET"]

    *(****CHAYA**** holds a wrapped cloth – a sleeping baby – and rocks it gently.)*

THE MARKET IS EMPTY
THE BUTCHER'S GONE HOME
THE CANDLE'S HALF SPENT,
SOON THE LIGHT WILL BE GONE

SOFTEN YOUR BROW DEAR,
BREATHE SLOW AND DEEP
LET YOUR EYES CLOSE AS YOU
DRIFT OFF TO SLEEP

THE MOON IN A WINDOW
THE SUN IN THE SEA
NOW IS THE QUIET
JUST BABY AND ME

AND THE SUN WILL SLEEP
IN THE OCEAN TONIGHT
AND THE COOL OF THE WATER
MAKES EVERYTHING RIGHT

AND THE OCEAN ONCE DREAMED
IT COULD SHINE HIGH ABOVE
BUT PROTECTING REFLECTING THE SUN
IS ENOUGH

    *(Lights shift away from **CHAYA**.)*

WE USED TO GO DANCING

    *(The performer is now both **CHAYA** and a musician, singing with **THE WANDERER**. The baby is gone.)*

THE WANDERER & CHAYA.

WE USED TO DRINK WINE
WE USED TO BUY FLOWERS
AND NOW WE BUY TIME

MOMMY AND DADDY
WOULD WORK BARE OUR HANDS
TO MAKE SURE YOU HAVE
ALL YOU NEED IN THIS LAND

THE WANDERER.   **CHAYA.**

THE MOON IN A WINDOW   OOH
THE SUN IN THE SEA   AAH

THE WANDERER & CHAYA.

NOW IS THE QUIET
JUST BABY AND ME

AND THE SUN WILL SLEEP
IN THE OCEAN TONIGHT
AND THE COOL OF THE WATER
MAKES EVERYTHING RIGHT

AND THE OCEAN ONCE DREAMED
IT COULD SHINE HIGH ABOVE
BUT PROTECTING REFLECTING THE SUN
IS ENOUGH

AND THE SUN WILL SLEEP
IN THE OCEAN TONIGHT
AND THE COOL OF THE WATER
MAKES EVERYTHING RIGHT

AND THE OCEAN ONCE DREAMED
IT COULD SHINE HIGH ABOVE
BUT PROTECTING REFLECTING THE SUN
IS ENOUGH

THE WANDERER.

PROTECTING
REFLECTING THE SUN
IS ENOUGH

(Lighting shift.)

Intermezzo Five

[MUSIC NO. 08A "THE ROAD TO RUSSIA"]

THE WANDERER. I'm reminded of an old lullaby I used to hear.

Well-known Jewish lullaby, it goes like this (I'll try to translate it for you):

> *(Beat.)*

It's cold
We're hungry
You'll probably starve...
Go to sleep.

> *(He sighs, nostalgically.)*

So okay
Romania
Chaya got out *before* it was too late
Chaim got out *after* it was too late
So Chaim looks forward because there's no looking back
But Chaya?
The cold of Canada still feels cold
The house is cold
The bed is cold.

> *(Beat.)*

> *(Lights come up on **CHAYA**, sitting, holding a baby.)*

When Chaim and Chaya's baby emerges from the womb
His eyes are closed and he doesn't cry and in the moment that he hangs suspended over Chaya before he's placed in her arms
Chaya sees herself on the road to Russia

> *(Lights shift. **CHAYA** is on the road to Russia.)*

Her husband died on that road

Chaya was five months along when he said his last words

They had so little food by then

Chaya's bones showed

Her skin sagged

Her stomach stuck out over her skinny legs

Her family passed her pieces of their bread but when her baby was born

Her milk didn't come

She gave the baby sugar water and whispered "stay, stay, you should stay" but it died

As is the custom, it wasn't mourned

Its grave wasn't marked

> *(Beat.)*

> *(Lights shift.* **CHAYA** *is in Montreal with her new baby.)*

Back in Canada, the new baby, still wet and blue, is placed in Chaya's arms

He opens his eyes

They're dark and full of knowledge

And for the first time in this big cold county, Chaya feels some warmth.

> *(Beat.)*

> *(There is the sound of thunder.)*

It's raining.

> *(Lights shift us to the next scene.)*

Scene Six

[MUSIC NO. 08B "IT'S RAINING"]

(**CHAYA** *holds the baby.*)

(**CHAIM** *hovers in the doorway, then tentatively steps into the room.*)

CHAYA. Your son.

> (*Beat.*)

CHAIM. His eyes.

> (*Beat.*)

He looks like me, may no more harm befall him!

> (*Beat.*)

Can I hold him?

CHAYA. No.

CHAIM. I can't?

CHAYA. No.

> (*Beat.*)

CHAIM. Your family are downstairs: all of them, seventeen people in the front room.

> (**CHAYA** *shoots him a look.*)

Nice of them to come.

> (*Beat.*)

Is there pain?

> (**CHAYA** *shrugs.*)

CHAYA. Ehn!

CHAIM. All night your father, and your brothers, they sat in the kitchen with me: we were drinking, telling jokes... It was a nice celebration except the whole time you were screaming.

> (*Beat.*)

I didn't like hearing you scream like that.

(Beat.)

What are we going to name him?

> (**CHAYA** *doesn't answer or acknowledge the question.*)

I was thinking after one of my brothers: Samuel.

CHAYA. He died young?

CHAIM. Yes.

CHAYA. Pogrom?

> (**CHAIM** *nods.*)

No one who died in a pogrom. What about after your father?

CHAIM. No.

CHAYA. Also pogrom?

> (**CHAYA** *looks up at him.*)

> (*But* **CHAIM** *doesn't answer or look at her.*)

No one?

> (**CHAYA** *considers him with new empathy.*)

> (*She hands him the baby.*)

Here.

> (**CHAIM** *looks down at his son.*)

Samuel?

> (**CHAIM** *nods.*)

CHAIM. Sam.

CHAYA. *(To herself.)* Sam.

CHAIM. *(To the baby.)* May you study Torah. May God hear you and may he answer you. And may you live to be an old man.

CHAYA. Amen.

> (*Lights shift to* **THE WANDERER.***)*

[MUSIC NO. 09 "FLEDGLING"]

THE WANDERER.

ONCE THERE WAS A MAMA BIRD WHO FLEW ACROSS THE SEA
CARRYING HER FLEDGLING YOUNG ALOFT UPON THE BREEZE

THE TIME HAD COME TO MIGRATE AS A CHILL FELL ON THE LAND
THE FLEDGLINGS WERE TOO WEAK TO FLY, TOO YOUNG TO UNDERSTAND

MAMA TOOK THEM ON HER BACK THE THREE INTO THE SKY
AND SET UPON HER JOURNEY WITH A PRAYER A SIGH

MAMA WHERE DO WE FLY?
WHERE ARE WE WELCOME
AND WHERE WILL WE THRIVE?

MAMA WHERE DO WE FLY?
WHERE ARE WE GOING
AND WILL WE SURVIVE?

THE JOURNEY WAS EXHAUSTING BUT AT LAST A SHORE WAS FOUND
THE FLEDGLINGS LEAPT OFF MAMA AS SHE CRASHED INTO THE GROUND

IT TOOK SOME TIME TO LEARN HOW TO ADAPT TO THE NEW CLIME
BUT FOOD WAS FOUND AND SHELTER AND IT FELT STABLE IN TIME
THE FAMILY WAS GRATEFUL TO SURVIVE ANOTHER DAY
BUT THEY MISSED THE LIFE THEY'D HAD AND ALL THEIR FRIENDS SO FAR AWAY

MAMA WHERE DO WE FLY?
WHERE ARE WE WELCOME
AND WHERE WILL WE THRIVE?

MAMA WHERE DO WE FLY?
WHERE ARE WE GOING
AND WILL WE SURVIVE?

Chaim and Chaya are noooowwwww:

Canadian!

Canadian, wouldn't you say?

Maybe not full Canadian but two thirds? Half?

That baby is Canadian: that baby is going to grow up shovelling snow!

Every fucking year for four fucking months fucking car fucking knee deep in snow.

Fuck!

Fuck you, snow!

Canadian?!!!

Canadian, yes?

Maybe not *old stock* Canadian, but Canadian?

AS YEARS PASSED OTHER FAMILIES FROM OTHER FAR OFF
    LANDS

BEGAN TO CROSS THE OCEAN AND TO WASH UP ON THE
    SAND

THE FLEDGELINGS AND THEIR NEIGHBOURS FELT
    THEMSELVES TO BE AS ONE

AND SCARCELY COULD IDENTIFY AS WITH NEW BIRDS ON
    THE RUN

THEY FEARED THAT ALL THE NEW BIRDS WOULD BRING
    VIOLENCE AND DISEASE

DESPITE AN OLD FAMILIAR SONG ALOFT UPON THE
    BREEZE

MAMA WHERE DO WE FLY?

WHERE ARE WELCOME

AND WHERE WILL WE THRIVE?

MAMA WHERE DO WE FLY?

WHERE ARE WE GOING

AND WILL WE SURVIVE?

    (Lights shift.)

[MUSIC NO. 09A "AND HERE'S THE CRACK AGAIN"]

Scene Seven

*(***CHAIM*** *comes into an empty room. He holds a brown package.)*

CHAIM. Chaya?

(Beat.)

Chaya? I passed a toy store and I got a little thing for Sam! And sugar! Sugar for you!

(Beat.)

I'm sorry – the storm slowed me down: I went into the toy store to get out of the storm and then I...

*(***CHAYA*** *comes in holding a bundle that is Sam. She's distressed.)*

What's wrong?

CHAYA. There's a rash on his stomach.

(Beat.)

CHAIM. A rash.

CHAYA. It – it – it's Typhus. It looks like what Yochay had and look –

*(***CHAYA*** *shows him the baby.)*

– his fingers are curled up –

CHAIM. Fever?

CHAYA. And his arms: look he's not lifting them.

CHAIM. He needs a doctor –

CHAYA. *(Fury.)* I know he needs a doctor!!!! I took him to the doctor: he wouldn't open the door!!!!!

CHAIM. He...? Why not?

CHAYA. I DON'T KNOW! He wouldn't let me in, he knew I was standing there, and he...wouldn't open the door.

(They both look down at Sam.)

I keep holding milk to his mouth but he won't drink it spills out...

(Beat.)

My father was here yesterday and I saw a rash on his neck and I thought that looks like Typhus and I...

(Beat.)

...thought it isn't Typhus God wouldn't...

(Beat.)

I cursed him.

CHAIM. He's sick because he's sick.

CHAYA. No I cursed him.

CHAIM. Did you curse your father? No. Then why does your father have a rash? It's not a curse, Chaya; it's Typhus.

(Beat.)

I'll go get a doctor.

CHAYA. Yes.

CHAIM. Can I hold him? Then I'll go.

> *(**CHAYA** hands him Sam and **CHAIM** holds him so very gently, in his arms...)*

> *(**CHAIM** whispers a prayer under his breath.)*

Mi Sheberakh. Avoteinu: Avraham, Yitzhak, v'Yaakov –

> *(As **CHAIM** looks down at his son, there is a shift.)*

THE WANDERER. And here's the crack again
Chaim looks down and sees his youngest brother in his arms
He's standing in his kitchen in Romania
"What happened to him?" Chaim asks his father
"They swung his head against the wall."

> *(The cymbals ring, jarring.)*

Chaim closes his eyes for a second
He knew the answer
He saw the blackened and beat in faces of his mother and brothers in the front room but he had to ask so he could see the grinning men pick his brother up and

(The cymbals ring, jarring.)

Chaim helps his father to his feet

Carrying his little brother in his arms and holding up his father he slowly walks out into the street towards the small hospital

The hospital is packed and they stand and wait until a nurse comes over and looks at the little boy's wounds and without stopping grabs the child and runs with him towards a doctor

The doctor

His arms in blood up to his armpits stitches the little boy up

Then lays him on a blanket in the corridor

Chaim holds his hand for hours

When he opens his eyes he looks up at Chaim

He says "where am I" and "why does my voice sound like this?"

Chaim tells him it's because he's missing some teeth

The little boy's eyes are clear and

Trusting

But ten hours later he dies on the floor of the dirty hospital

Chaim and his father walk back home with the little boy's body wrapped up in a blanket

In the cold house, Chaim's father finds a pocket razor and without a word to Chaim

Slits his own neck

(The cymbals ring, jarring.)

Chaim lays them all out in the front room

His father, his mother, and his four brothers

Elijah, Daveed, Benesh

And the youngest

Sam.

CHAIM. Amen.

CHAYA. Go, go: get a doctor.

CHAIM. Pray for him.

CHAYA. *(Nodding.)* Go.

> (**CHAIM** *goes out quickly.*)

> (*Once* **CHAIM** *is gone,* **CHAYA** *holds the baby in her arms. She rocks back and forwards as she says the following prayer.*)

May the one who blessed our ancestors, Abraham, Isaac and Jacob, bless and heal Samuel Moscovitch, my son, may the Holy One strengthen him and heal him soon...

> (*Emotion makes it difficult for her to speak so she stops speaking. Pulls herself together and starts over.*)

May the one who blessed our ancestors, Abraham, Isaac and Jacob, bless and heal Samuel Moscovitch, my son, may the Holy One strengthen him and...

> (*Again, emotion makes it difficult to speak.*)

May you – may you...please...please...

> (*Now* **THE WANDERER** *walks towards* **CHAYA**. **CHAYA** *doesn't see him but as soon as* **THE WANDERER** *is close to her she feels his presence.* **THE WANDERER** *takes off his tallis and lays it around her shoulders. He looks towards her with great compassion. Though* **CHAYA** *doesn't see him, she feels his warmth.*)

God?

> (*Lighting shift.*)

Intermezzo Six

(**THE WANDERER** *grabs a microphone and walks towards the audience, up close to them.*)

THE WANDERER. You guys all right out there?

It's getting dark

It's getting a little dark

The laughs are turning into "why the fuck did I come and see this depressing show"

I hope you're not getting too depressed

But if you are getting too depressed, remember: none of this really happened. This isn't real.

It's just a story.

(**THE WANDERER** *smiles, sadly.*)

That's a lie.

(*Lighting shift to.*)

[MUSIC NO. 10 "EL MALEI RACHAMIM"]

(*Wrapped in a tallis and holding a prayer book,* **THE WANDERER** *sings ad-lib.*)

EL MALEH RACHAMIM,

SHOCHAYN BAM'ROMIM,

HAM-TZAY M'NUCHA N'CHONA TACHAS KANFAY
    HASH'CHINA,

B'MA-ALOS K'DOSHIM UT-HORIM K'ZO-HAR HARAKI-A
    MAZHIRIM,

ES NISHMAS "YANKEL BEN-YISROEL" SHE-HOLEYCH
    L-OYLAMO,

B'GAN AYDEN B'GAN AYDEN T'HAY M'NUCHASO;

ANA: LA-CHAYN BA-AL HARACHAMIM YAS-TIRE-HU
    B'SAYSER K'NAFAV L'OLAMIM, V'YITZ-ROR BITZ-ROR

HACHA-YIM ES NISHMASOH,

ADO-NAY HU NA-CHALOSOH,

V'YANU-ACH B'SHALOM OY B'SHALOM AL MISHKAVOH.

V'NOMAR, V'NOMAR, V'NOMAR: AMAYN.

(*Lighting shifts us to the next scene.*)

Scene Eight

[MUSIC NO. 10A "HIS FEVER'S GONE"]

(**CHAIM** *sleeps in a chair.* **CHAYA** *comes – walks across the stage – and kneels in front of him.*)

CHAYA. Chaim.

(**CHAIM** *wakes up.*)

His fever's gone.

(*Beat.*)

CHAIM. It's gone.

(**CHAYA** *nods, then.*)

CHAYA. He slept, and while he slept his skin got colder: I thought it was...death, but it wasn't, because he woke up and ate bread and milk, and didn't seem so sick, and I realized what I thought was death was his fever going away.

(**CHAIM** *shows his relief.*)

(*Head sinks into his hands.*)

CHAIM. When did I fall asleep? I would have sat with him –

CHAYA. You were tired and I was with him.

CHAIM. I'll go up – you can go to your family. Tell them – Chaya...tell them I am...so sorry about your father.

CHAYA. Yes.

(**CHAYA** *goes towards the door.*)

(*Before she can go out...*)

CHAIM. You're a good mother. And a good wife.

CHAYA. I'm not a good wife.

CHAIM. Sometimes you're not.

(**CHAYA** *looks at him, then quickly looks away.*)

CHAYA. I told you: find a young bride.

CHAIM. I didn't like the young brides I met with, and I remembered you, and your look, and how you were very serious, and how when I spoke to you I knew I'd find a place for myself in Canada. Then I came to Montreal and I met with young brides and they asked me if I liked music and if I liked dogs and if I liked rainbows. They didn't know anything about life.

>   *(Beat.)*

CHAYA. I was a good wife to Yochay, but I'm not...

>   *(Beat.)*

...the same now...

CHAIM. No.

>   *(Beat.)*

Probably not.

CHAYA. You want from me what I had to give to Yochay but...

>   *(**CHAIM** nods, understanding her.)*

I can't remember not knowing him, I picked flowers for him, I went to shul just to look at him, he said his last words to me...

>   *(**CHAYA** shakes her head, doesn't know what else to say. Slowly, **CHAIM** walks towards her.)*

CHAIM. You're going to love Yochay all your life. Good, fine, I won't ask you to stop: how can you stop? But can you love him and me too?

>   *(Lighting shift to* **THE WANDERER.***)*

[MUSIC NO. 11 "WHAT LOVE CAN HEARTBREAK ALLOW?"]

THE WANDERER.

>   A TANGLE OF TRAUMAS
>   A RASH OF REGRETS
>   A BUNDLE OF BURDENSOME YESTERDAYS

A BLESSING OF SORROWS
A CRUSH OF TOMORROWS
A NIGHTMARE DISTURBED BY THE DAWN;

A QUORUM OF TRAGEDY
ROTTEN MENAGERIE
WHY DO YOU STAY WITH ME NOW?

A TIDE OF NAÎVITE
DRAGGING THE FEET OF ME
WHAT LOVE CAN HEARTBREAK ALLOW?

THE WANDERER.	CHAIM.
WHEN I WAS A CHILD	A TANGLE OF TRAUMAS, A RASH OF REGRETS,
I DREAMED OF ALL OF THE THINGS I'D BE;	A BUNDLE OF BURDENSOME YESTERDAYS;
NOW IT'S ALL GONE WILD AND THERE'S A CRACK IN MY HISTORY;	A BLESSING OF SORROWS A CRUSH OF TOMORROWS A NIGHTMARE DISTURBED BY THE DAWN;
WHERE SHALL I RETURN NOW THAT ALL MY BEGINNINGS HAVE BURNED? WHAT OF ALL MY DREAMS?	A QUORUM OF TRAGEDY ROTTEN MENAGERIE, WHY DO YOU STAY WITH NOW? A TIDE OF NAÎVITE DRAGGING THE FEET OF ME;

THE WANDERER & CHAIM.

WHAT LOVE CAN HEARTBREAK ALLOW?

THE WANDERER.	CHAIM.	CHAYA.
NOW THE WINTER'S OVER	WHEN I WAS A CHILD	A TANGLE OF TRAUMAS, A RASH OF REGRETS,
AND THE STORM HAS PASSED,	I DREAMED OF ALL OF THE THINGS	A BUNDLE OF BURDENSOME

THE WANDERER.	**CHAIM.**	**CHAYA.**
THE RAIN'S RECEDED;	I'D BE;	YESTERDAYS;
FLOWERS GROW	NOW	A BLESSING OF SORROWS
UPON THE EARTH,	IT'S ALL GONE WILD AND THERE'S	A CRUSH OF TOMORROWS,
THE TIME TO LOVE IS HERE;	A CRACK IN MY HISTORY;	A NIGHTMARE DISTURBED BY THE DAWN;
I OPENED UP TO MY BELOVED	WHERE SHALL I RETURN, NOW THAT	A QUORUM OF TRAGEDY ROTTEN MENAGERIE,
BUT MY LOVE HAD TURNED AWAY;	ALL MY BEGINNINGS HAVE BURNED?	WHY DO YOU STAY WITH ME NOW?
I CALLED HIM, BUT HE GAVE NO ANSWER;	WHAT OF ALL MY DREAMS?	A TIDE OF NAÎVITE DRAGGING THE FEET OF ME;

THE WANDERER, CHAIM & CHAYA.

WHAT LOVE CAN HEARTBREAK ALLOW?

CHAIM & CHAYA.

NOW THE WINTER'S OVER
AND THE STORM HAS PASSED,
THE RAIN'S RECEDED;
FLOWERS GROW UPON THE EARTH
THE TIME TO LOVE IS HERE;
I OPENED UP TO MY BELOVED
BUT MY LOVE HAD TURNED AWAY;
I CALLED HIM BUT HE GAVE NO ANSWER;

WHAT LOVE CAN HEARTBREAK ALLOW?
WHAT LOVE CAN HEARTBREAK ALLOW?

THE WANDERER.

WHAT LOVE CAN HEARTBREAK ALLOW?

(Lighting shift.)

Intermezzo Seven

THE WANDERER. Let me tell you a story

You're in the kitchen

For hours now you've been telling yourself to stop answering e-mails and go to bed

You get up to turn out the lights

And someone knocks on your back door

It's the middle of the night

No one's supposed to be coming by...?

It's weird how much that made you jump because someone who wanted to break in wouldn't knock, would they?

And that's when they knock again

It's hard to tell if the knocking is urgent or

There's a little window in the kitchen that gives you an obscured view of the backyard

So you go closer and there *is* a person standing there

Of course there is – someone knocked

You can't see them you can only see their shadow but

They're standing very still

You call through the door "hello hi"

They don't answer

But then you did winterize these windows and the door is made of solid oak it wouldn't surprise you if they couldn't hear

There's only one of you...

You want to be practical

You don't want to wind up face down in a ditch

But you do want to

Help if it's a person who needs help.

You're standing there with your hand on the deadbolt...

You hear a sound

It's something...rustling

You look down and see a small piece of paper slowly being pushed under the door

Which freaks you out
But you bend down and look it at
And there's nothing on it
And you think "that's fucking...not helpful"
You turn the piece of paper over in your hand as you're
going over all this and there's the writing
On the back
It's not in English
And you think
Fuck!
Or maybe it's scrawled so badly that it looks like it's not
in English
Fuck!
Maybe it says: "I'm hurt" or "I need help" or
"you're dead"
What do you do?
Do you open the door?

  (Lighting shift.)

Scene Nine

[MUSIC NO. 11A "BEH SHA'AH TOVAH"]

(**CHAIM** *comes in.* **CHAYA** *gazes at him.*)

(*He pants, overheated, gazing back at her. He can't catch his breath. Can't speak.*)

CHAYA. Hard day at work?

CHAIM. (*Nods.*) Hhhhyyeh…

(**CHAYA** *gazes at her husband.*)

(*There's a sexual charge to the gaze.*)

(**CHAYA** *makes a tiny motion towards him.*)

(**CHAIM** *clocks it and goes to her and kisses her.*)

(*But then they don't know quite what to do: awkward.*)

CHAYA. I'll get dinner.

(**CHAIM** *nods.*)

CHAIM. Yes.

(*Beat.*)

CHAYA. The neighbours lent Sam a sled.

(*Beat.*)

(*Smiling.*) We're out of sugar.

(*Beat.*)

CHAIM. Chaya?

CHAYA. I think…

(**CHAIM** *turns and looks at her.*)

I think you're going to be a father again.

(*Beat.*)

Yes!

CHAIM. Mazel Tov!

CHAYA. Mazel Tov!

CHAIM. Beh Sha'ah tovah.

>(**CHAYA** *laughs.*)

>(*Pause.*)

Do you...still think of Romania?

>(**CHAYA** *shrugs.*)

CHAYA. Enh!

>(*Beat.*)

The people here are nice to Sam. And my father. I wouldn't want an ocean between me and his grave.

>(*They smile at each other.*)

>(*Lights shift subtly as* **THE WANDERER** *says the below words.*)

THE WANDERER. (*To the audience.*) Chaya and Chaim have four children, Sam Moscovitch, Michal Moscovitch, Saul Moscovitch, and Ethel Moscovitch.

CHAIM. I got them all bicycles.

CHAYA. Why?

CHAIM. So they can bicycle?

THE WANDERER. (*To the audience.*) Sam Moscovitch's bar mitzvah is held at the Shaar Hashomayim Synagogue in Montreal on De Bullion Street.

CHAYA. (*Crying.*) Good looking boy, like you were.

CHAIM. He wanted me to teach him to shave. I said to him: you have no moustache hair what are you going to shave off? Your skin?

What – what's wrong with you?

CHAYA. I'm crying?

THE WANDERER. (*To the audience.*) Sam Moscovitch fights for Canada in World War Two – against the axis powers Germany, Italy, Japan, and Romania – and is awarded the Canadian Volunteer Medal for his service.

CHAYA. He's on the telephone! Chaim! Pick up the telephone!

CHAIM. What!

CHAYA. Sam's on the phone!!!! He's bringing a girl to Shabbas, her name is Sally. What kind of a name is *Sally*?

THE WANDERER. *(To the audience.)* Sam Moscovitch marries Sally Grenofsky and they have two children, Allan Moscovitch and Enid Moscovitch.

CHAIM. You know what I did today? I told Allan and Enid about Brasov, and the kosher market, and the synagogue with the stained glass –

CHAYA. You know what I did today? I fixed your shorts so wear your shorts.

CHAIM. I don't like those shorts.

CHAYA. I bought you those shorts so you *like* those shorts whether you like those shorts or not.

THE WANDERER. *(To the audience.)* Sam's son, Allan Moscovitch, is the first in the family to go to University.

CHAIM. Chaya! Chaya!! Allan got into McGill!!!!! Full scholarship!

THE WANDERER. *(To the audience.)* Chaya dies in 1955, in Montreal, of heart failure at the age of seventy-seven. Chaim lives until 1975 and dies at the age of ninety-two, an old man. Chaim and Chaya have eight grandchildren and sixteen great-grandchildren. Last year, their fourteenth great-great-grandchild was born, a boy: Elijah.

> *(***CHAYA** *and* **CHAIM** *turn and look directly at* **THE WANDERER.***)*

> *(The three of them smile at each other.)*

(To **CHAIM** *and* **CHAYA.***)* Mazel Tov.

> *(***CHAIM** *and* **CHAYA** *nod their thanks.)*

> *(Lighting shift to the next scene.)*

Intermezzo Eight

WANDERER. Alright! We made it, you made it, others were not so lucky.

Others *are* not so lucky.

[MUSIC NO. 12 "MY ANGELS"]

(Beat.)

Okay New York*, it's time for us to pack it up and ship ourselves off to the next town, we hope they'll be as kind and hospitable as you've been, we hope they'll let us in, we hope they'll look past our "barbaric cultural practices" to see our shared humanity and open their doors to us.

(Beat.)

But before we go, Ladies and Gentlemen and those who identify outside the binary, I'd like to introduce to you... My Angels.

Playing Chaim and woodwinds, _____

Playing the drums and the cymbals, _____

Playing keyboards and the accordion, _____

Playing Chaya and violin, _____

I have been The Wanderer!

[MUSIC NO. 13 "THE WANDERER'S BULGAR (REPRISE)"]

It's been an honour and a privilege to be with you here *tonight!*

> (**THE WANDERER** *and* **CHAYA** *dance. They close the doors to the shipping container, with themselves inside.)*

> *(As the music ends, the trap door opens at the top of the shipping container opens and* **THE WANDERER** *waves to the audience.)*

The End

---

* Insert the name of the town where the show is happening tonight.